Special Operations Vampire Elimination Unit

P. J. Kearns

Paul J Kearns

ISBN:9781072967811

FOR CARRIE, QUINN AND ERIN,
And all my family and friends.

ACKNOWLEDGMENTS

Thank you to Carrie, Quinn and Erin for all your love and support.

Thank you to my Mum, Dad for bring me up right, for teaching me

that I can shape my own future, and teaching me to go and get what I want from life.

Thank you to Noel and Sam for the ongoing support and believing in me,

Thank you to my cousin Louise Croft for your editing notes (I did the final editing so if it's still wrong on my head be it.)

Thank you to all my extended family for being there when we have needed you most and for being amazing.

Thank you to all my friends, you know who you are and know I love you.

Fletcher's Preparations.

Sergeant Major John Fletcher set up the room for the forthcoming interviews. One hundred and nineteen soldiers had applied for the six available places. He was the Head Science Officer of the S.O.V.E.U. and as Sergeant Major he was more than qualified to take on this role of interviewer.

The applicants had been whittled down to the final fourteen. Over the past three days they had been through a strict medical evaluation, a fitness test, a mental proficiency evaluation and a weapons proficiency test. This interview was the final stage on their assessment. These final fourteen were applying not only to be part of the Special Operations: Vampire Elimination Unit. The role was also to be part of Andra Hudson's own personal attack team.

He took the pile of soldier's profile folders from his briefcase and placed them on his right hand side of the desk. He made sure that they were in corresponding order. It would save him time later on as he wouldn't have to search for the file to go with each interviewee. He made sure all his pens worked and set two trays down on his left hand side of the desk.

You couldn't be just regular Army to get into the S.O.V.E.U. You had to be a career soldier of at least ten years. You had to have seen active service within a Special Forces unit. Finally you had to have had 'experienced' a certain type of enemy to qualify you to get to this stage.

He looked at his watch. It was one minute to nine on the 18th March 2016. He drank the last mouthful of his coffee, straightened his suit and made sure his buttons shined. Only then did he approach the door. He took one last look at his watch and as the numbers changed to 9:00 he opened to door. There sat a nervous looking interviewee. Fletcher smiled him.

"Mr Smith. Please come in," he said.

Steven White interview.

Steven White sat in the waiting room. He had got here fifteen minutes before his interview appointment. He was eager and in his own honest opinion a little bit nervous. This wasn't just any old interview, it was for a place in the S.O.V.E.U. A top secret military unit. They were highly specialised and extremely tough. His superior officer had green lit him for this interview two months ago.

He sat on the edge of his seat leaning forwards with the fingers of both hands pressed tip to tip. Almost in a subconscious prayer. He looked at his watch. It was five to ten. Five minutes to go. He looked down at himself. He polished his buttons with a handkerchief, gave his boots a quick buff and checked his tie. He then checked his reflection in the glass panel in the door to the waiting room. The room on the other side of it was low-lit so it served as a makeshift mirror. His white hair was short and neat and his light blue eyes showed nothing of the almost sleepless night he had had prior to this morning's interview. Everything was fine, he was just being over-cautious. The door opened and a woman walked out. She too was dressed in military uniform. An officer followed her out.

"Mr. White. Please come in," he said.

Steven got to his feet, straightened his jacket and followed him. The room was light and airy. There was a two way mirror on one side, a big window on the other and a door at the other end of the room. A long pine desk stood in the middle of the room. On one side of the desk there was a pile of files. On the other side there were two trays. One marked yes and the other marked no. There was already two files in the no tray. The officer walked behind the desk and offered the chair on the other side to Steven.

"I'm Sergeant Major Fletcher. Please sit down, Mr. White."

"Thank you Sir," said Steven and sat down in the chair.

Fletcher then took a file from the top of the pile and opened it. There was a picture of Steven at the top left corner. Inside was information about every mission Steven White had ever worked.

"I see you have signed the Official Secrets Act," said Fletcher.

"Yes Sir," said Steven.

"Ok good. I am required by law to tell you that everything you see and hear in this room today stays in this room. If you tell anyone about anything you see or we discuss it will result in an instant court martial and dismissal from all military forces, is that understood?"

"Yes Sir."

"Ok. We'll begin then, White. You don't mind to be referred to by your surname do you?"

"No Sir."

"For the record please state your full name, regiment, and where you are from," said Fletcher.

"Steven John White. British Army Sniper regiment. I'm from Leeds, West Yorkshire in England."

"Thank you. How long have you been in the armed forces?"

"In brief I joined the regular army at eighteen. I completed my basic training then at the age of nineteen in 2001 and joined the sniper regiment. I did my training and was posted to Afghanistan. I did three tours of active service there and two months ago I came back from my second tour of Iraq. So sixteen years all together."

"When did you first hear about the S.O.V.E.U.?"

"Four months ago. Eight months into my second tour of Iraq. I had to give my commanding officer a report about the incident there."

"The incident? Can you elaborate on that?"

"Er... yes of course Sir," he looked at the floor and was quiet for a second. When he looked back up and began to speak again. "It was five months ago. 15th October 2015. My outfit were on a night manoeuvre. It was all going to plan. We had tracked a group of Taliban fighters to a hideout two miles outside the green zone. We suspected they were running a human trafficking racket. Our ground soldiers moved in and surrounded the building. I was half a mile away on a cliff in an armoured Land Rover Defender recon vehicle with my 338 Lapua sniper rifle. I took out the two guards on the roof with one round and the soldiers move in. They engaged the Taliban inside the building in heavy gun fire. Then over the radio came these growls and roars. That's when my outfit began to scream. I had heard people get shot before, blown up too but I had never heard anything like this. It sounded like they were being torn apart. There were screams and cries of pain and torture. I shot out some of the windows in an attempt to get a visual on some targets. There was something covering the windows though. Whatever it was held them together. I couldn't differentiate between my soldiers and the Taliban. I couldn't just shoot blindly into the building. I didn't want to hit the members of my outfit. The screaming died down. I then saw some movement on the roof. Six figures, they were dressed like Taliban but they weren't. They looked like humans but they moved in a strange way."

"Can you explain what you mean by strange?" said Fletcher.

"Yes Sir. They were fast. Like they had been sped up. Not like in old films but in an unnatural way. There was something not quite human about them. On top of that they would switch from walking upright to on all fours like apes. I chose my target and fired. A clean headshot. Should have been an instant kill but the thing stumbled about for a second before it fell. I prepared to choose my next target when I noticed they had all stopped moving. They were all looking right at me. One of them opened its mouth and let out a high pitched howl. I got it in my scope and shot it through the base of its skull via its open mouth. The other four leapt from the roof of the building and came running at us. I have never seen any kind of animal move so fast. I tried to target them but they alternated their path so fast I could hardly keep up. They were closing us down at an incredible rate. I screamed at Jonesy to move. He didn't wait to see them. He just put his foot down. I put down my sniper rifle and picked up my custom AK 47. I was shooting from the back of the vehicle as we sped away. I hit them I know I did but it didn't seem to matter. One of them jumped onto the car, pushed his head into the open back window, looked me right in the eye and roared. Its then that I noticed the long sharp teeth. He grabbed my shoulder and pulled me towards those teeth. I forced the barrel of my gun into his jaws and let rip. His thrashing, headless body fell from the back of the car. I watched the clumps of his skull that had fallen into the car burn and turn to ash. The other three were trying to tear their way into the car. We weren't far from the base when one of them forced their arm in and took hold of Jonesy. I pulled out my knife and stabbed repeatedly. It's generally not considered a good idea to shoot a gun inside an armoured vehicle of any sort. Eventually it let go and we arrived back at base. The three monsters fled off into the darkness. I now know they were vampires."

"That was a close encounter. You were lucky to survive," said Fletcher.

"A bit too bloody close if you ask me Sir. Sorry Sir, excuse my language," said White.

"No, please. Don't worry about it. This isn't the regular Army. We like our soldiers to speak their minds. It allows for input and faster thought and reaction times. Would you be willing to fight against vampires again?"

"Yes Sir. Those bastards took out my entire outfit. I'd kill every last one of them if I could."

"Good. Good, that is the reaction I was hoping for. Ok White. That is all."

White stood up with Fletcher.

"Thank you for this opportunity Sir," he said and turned to leave.

"Come this way please. We have another waiting room. There are refreshments, amenities and entertainment. It's a lot more comfortable than the one out there," said Fletcher.

He then led White through the door at the far end of the room.

Helen Davis Interview.

Helen Davis was prompt and on time for her eleven o'clock interview. Her hair was neat, she had no makeup on and nor did she need it. Born of a Hispanic mother and a Jamaican father, she was an exquisite beauty. Her light brown skin was flawless. Her suit was tidy and clean. Her hazel eyes scanned the magazines on the table as she made sure her hair was tidy. Not even thirty seconds after she had sat down Fletcher opened the door and let out the previous interviewee.

"You must be Helen Davis?" he said.

"Yes I am, Sir," she said.

"Ok. Come through please."

She stood up and followed him into the interview room. He stood behind the desk.

"I'm Sergeant Major Fletcher. Please sit down, Miss Davis," he said and gestured towards the chair on the other side of the desk.

She walked in and sat down. He picked her file off the pile and opened it. All the interviewee's files all had the same layout. There was a picture of Helen in the top left corner. Inside was information about every mission she had ever worked.

"You have signed the official secrets act?"

"I did, Sir."

"Ok good. I am required by law to tell you that everything you see and hear in this room today stays in this room. If you tell anyone about anything you see or anything we discuss it will result in an instant court martial and dismissal from all military forces, is that understood?"

"It is, Sir."

"First of all you don't mind if I refer to you by your surname from now on do you?"

"No, Sir. I'm used to being called Davis."

"Ok. Thank you, Davis. Let's begin. For the record please state your full name, regiment and where you are from. Then please tell me about your career in the armed forces."

"My name is Helen Melissa Davis. I'm an Explosive Device Deconstruction Technician in the U.S. Army Sir. I'm from Sacramento in California in the U.S.A. I signed up in 2002. I completed my basic training twelve weeks later. I was posted in Iraq for a ten month tour. While I was there a position in the bomb disposal regiment came up. I put my name down. I was one of only two of the original ten of us to complete the training and go through to the next stage. I was offered the position and took it. This is what I joined up for. I come from a town where not much happens Sir. I was there to work and that is what I did.
I successfully cleared seventy-six IEDs in that period. I went home for three months. I then did another two twelve month tours of Iraq and a twelve month tour of Afghanistan. That is why I earned the nickname 'Highlander'. Because of the film."

"Is that because of your encounter?"

"Yes Sir. Well, part of the reason. Not a lot of us in bomb disposal tend to live that long. And those of us that don't usually come back in one piece."

"Can you tell me about the incident please?"

"Of course Sir. It was 4th February 2016. We had a call out that an insurgent was in the process of planting a road side IED a mile outside Helmand Province. We set off to the location as the copter pilot had lost his visual on the guy. When we got there the sun hadn't risen but its light approached from over the horizon. I got out my flashlight, searched the area and found the site of disturbed ground. My team set up the lamps while I suited up. I slowly approached the site and began to uncover the area.

After digging for five minutes I still hadn't found anything. IEDs are usually only a few inches below the ground and I had already dug a foot down. My teammates told me to leave it. Sometimes the Insurgents dig fake holes to throw us off. I had a hunch though. Maybe I should have quit but it was then that I made the discovery. A human hand. I followed it up the arm to the chest. I thought I had found a body...until it moved. I had never seen anything like this. How could someone bury themselves this far down and still be alive.

The hand reached up and grabbed me by the throat. I tried to fight it but its strength was immense. The body then threw the remaining earth off of itself and sat up. It pulled me close and roared in my face. I didn't understand the language it spoke but I know it wasn't a local dialect. I punched it in the face to no effect. Still it held me by my throat it then stood up and took me with it. If it hadn't been for the suit it would have been choking me. It threw me at my team mates. I hit Barns and Wesker, knocked them over and landed on them. It then dragged Wesker from under me. Held him up and bit deep into his neck. Blood seeped from the sides of its mouth.

Wesker was dead in seconds. Barns and I shot at it and though the bullets tore its flesh it just kept on coming. It grabbed Barns and it...er...it pulled his head off with its bare hands, so easily. Like it was pulling a fucking chicken apart."

She stopped talking for a moment. Tears welled in her eyes but she blinked them away. She composed herself and continued.

"It picked me up and threw me at the front of the Vehicle. It then walked over and flipped it over and tore open the gas tank. It scrapped its claws over the underside sending sparks flying. One hit the gasoline and the whole thing went up. Somehow it moved out of the way before the flames could catch it. It then went back to the hole and began to dig trying to bury itself again. I stood up and threw myself at it and knocked it to the ground. I pushed my gun in its face and pulled the trigger three times. Blood poured from the wounds but they seemed to start healing in the same instance. It grabbed me by the throat and rolled over so it was on top of me. The anger in its eyes was horrifying. My vision began to fade. Just as I was about to pass out its skin began to bubble and then burn. It jumped off me and as I caught my breath I could see that the sun was coming up over the horizon. It was the sun that was burning it. I realised than that it must be a vampire. It seemed absurd but what else could it be. It screamed as it burned until it stood like a burnt wooden statue. I took out my phone and took a photo of it. Moments later its legs crumbled and it fell to the ground and shattered into dust.

That was it, I was alone out there. I've never felt so vulnerable in my life. I radioed the attack in and requested an urgent evac. I cried when I saw the car coming down the road.

When I got back I wrote a report and was offered unconditional leave for as long as I wanted. I didn't accept it as I felt I couldn't just walk away. That is when I was told about the S.O.V.E.U. That was six weeks ago and that brings us up to date."

"You do know that was a feral vampire you fought against?" Said Fletcher.

"So I have been told."

"I have only met one other person who has survived a feral vampire attack. They're rare and incredibly tough. With that I am going to offer you a place here on our team. If you are willing to accept, that is."

"Thank you Sir. Yes I accept."

"That concludes this interview. Thank you Davis."

He stood up and led her to the other door at the far end of the room.

"Please take a seat through here in the waiting room. There are refreshments, entertainment and amenities if you need them. My superior officer wants to see you later if you don't mind staying for a while."

"Yes that's fine. Thank you Sir."

She went through into the waiting room and sat down across from White.

Zarveya Hussain Interview.

Zarveya Hussain strode into the waiting room. She carried herself with an immense amount of confidence. She straightened her jacket and sat down. Her long black hair was tied in a ponytail and hung down her back between her narrow but strong shoulders. With her rounded face and cute features she could flash a sweet smile that was deceptive of the formidable soldier that she was. She was ten minutes early for her 13.30 pm interview. She sat back but didn't rest against the chair. She sat in quiet contemplation of the interview that would occur in the next ten minutes and closed her dark eye. She mentally went over everything. The clock reached half past one. Fletcher opened the door and let out the previous interviewee.

"Ms. Hussain?" he said.

"Yes, Sir," she said as she stood up in one fluid movement.

"Please come in," he said.
She walked into the room and over to the chair. She stood next to it and waited.

"I'm Sergeant Major Fletcher. Please sit down, Mrs. Hussain," he said.

"Thank you." She said and sat down.

"Ok let's begin," said Fletcher.
He then took her file from the top of the pile and opened it.

"You have signed the official secrets act?" said Fletcher.

"Yes Sir," said Zarveya.

"Good. I am required by law to tell you that everything you see and hear in this room today stays in this room. If you tell anyone about anything you see or we discuss it will result in an instant court martial and dismissal from all military forces, is that understood?"

"Yes Sir," said Zarveya.
She said it with so much force that Fletcher looked up from the file.

"At ease, soldier. This isn't the Armed forces. We are an independent military group. We work with the Armed Forces but we work in a different way. You can relax."

"So you're telling me you're a militia?"

"Of sorts." Smiled Fletcher. "Just a lot more organised and regulated. We work to reach an outcome that benefits the masses rather than the sole funder."

"I know you are vampire hunters but what is this outcome that will benefit the masses?"

"As our names suggest our aim is the elimination of vampires." Fletcher's face became serious. "Our main aim is to destroy every last vampire. We'll weed them out at the source."

"The source? So you believe that there is a lead vampire?"

"We don't just believe it. We have documented files. We have boxes full of physical evidence. We even have eye witness proof of his existence."

"If that is your aim I want to sign up."

"That is why you're here. First of all for the record please state your full name, regiment and where you are from. We need to know more information about you. When you joined the armed forces? What you have experienced that has lead you to us?"

"I am Zarveya Hussain. I am a close quarters and small arms ballistics expert. Specialising in deniable deep insertion operations. I was born just outside Mumbai in India in 1986.

When I was seven my family was attacked by an intruder in our fourth floor apartment. I had school the next day so I was in bed. My two younger sisters and I were woken by screams of terror from our mother and grandmother. The screams came from the main room. We quietly got out of bed sneaked into the hallway. I got my sisters to the apartment door. From behind us came a hideous laughter. I opened the door and made my sisters go first. A hand grabbed me by the shoulder. I screamed at my sisters to run and get help. I was then dragged back into the apartment and into the sitting room.

My father, grandfather and my older brother all lay dead on the floor. Their throats had been torn out. I was thrown like a doll at my mother. She caught me the best she could then lay down over me and covered me in a blanket.

I could hear a voice. It sounded like our landlord, Ginushku. I knew his voice as he had been to the apartment before and threatened my father about the rent.

'If you do not pay me what you owe me I will be back. I will take your daughters. They will bring a good price at the traders market,' he had said.

He would threaten my father with this as everyone knew that this meant slavery or prostitution. My father wanted neither for us. He wanted us to have good lives and educations. Now my father lay dead.

'I warned you, child. I told you all that if I didn't get my rent I would take it in other ways. It has been three months and I have not been paid.' I have found another way to take my payment. I have bought myself the eternal life of a blood drinker. I will take my payment from the veins of my tenants from now on. Starting with you and your family,' Ginushku said to me.

Then my grandmother screamed as he dragged her up from the floor. She beat at him with her fists but it was no use. He was far too strong. He grabbed her head and yanked it back.

'Say goodbye to your grandmother,' he said, relishing our fear.

My mother screamed and cursed at him. He sunk his teeth into my grandmother's throat and tore away the flesh then lapped at the blood that poured down her neck. Laughing as he did it. Her last weak breath gurgled from her lips as her lifeless body hit the floor with a thud. My mother screamed as he took hold of her hair and pulled her away from me. I screamed as her hand slipped away from mine. He held her there next to the pile of my family's bloodless bodies.

I sobbed for my mother as she looked at me.

'Do not be afraid my child. Remember me. Protect yourself,' she said.

Her voice was so calming that I could focus through the fear. I remembered the knitting needles. She had told us that if we were ever attacked to use our grandmother's knitting needles as weapons. I scurried around under the blanket and found one of them. I stood up and wrapped the blanket around myself with just my left arm uncovered. I walked over to the monster, Ginushku. As he pulled my mother's head back to expose her neck I reached my hand up to him and I pleaded with him.

'Please Sir. Don't hurt my mother. Please. Take my blood instead. Please don't hurt my mother.' He turned his head away from my mother's neck and looked down at me with a hideous smile. That is when the attack came. Not from me but from my mother. She swung all her weight into her right arm and stabbed the other knitting needle into his left eye. It hit him with such force that the tip of the needle pierced the other side of his head. He stumbled around and came towards me. I threw aside the blanket and thrust my needle into his right eye. From my height the needle went through his eyeball and into his brain. He cried out and now blinded he thrashed around wildly. My mother grabbed me and hauled me up to her chest and ran for the door. Just before we got to it my uncle Bealu kicked the door in. He was carrying his wood axe. My sisters had ran to his house and raised the alarm. He strode in, his huge frame nearly filled the entire door way.

'Go. Get her to safety,' he said. My mother ran out of the apartment but stood and watched from the hallway. Ginushku stumble towards my uncle. His arms outstretched and screaming. Bealu swung the axe up into the air and brought it down on Ginushku's skull, splitting his head in two. He stumbled about for a few moments.

Bealu hit him three more times before he fell. His body then smouldered like it was burning from the inside out and turned to ash.

We reported the attack to the police but it never really went any further. They didn't catch the people who had turned Ginushku into a vampire. The vampire network goes too deep for normal police to follow. Though they are taking money to turn people into vampires they can disappear in a day. If they don't want to be found the police will never find them. No one will ever talk either. Vampires can get to you in a way that no police force ever could. There is nowhere you can hide from vampires. My father, brother, grandfather, and grandmother were buried a few days later. It became known that I and my family were vampire killers. We were always scared that some of them would find us. We were hounded out of villages because people were scared of the horrors we might attract.

When I was nine my mother moved us here, to England. Life was safer. I went to school and got an education. At the age of eighteen, in 2004 I joined the army. I completed two tours of Afghanistan. It soon became clear to my superiors that I was willing to push myself harder than most. I put in applications to be considered for Special Forces and I was accepted. I worked my way up. I was involved in operations I am not allowed to disclose, not even to you. I am always trying to learn all I can about combat so that one day I might become a vampire hunter. This quest eventually brought your organisation to my attention. I had to search deep within military files to find any mention of you. Almost earning myself a court martial when I was caught poking my nose in files I had no clearance to be reading. When I was asked what the hell I thought I was doing I told them my story. I was pointed in this direction and here I am today."

"That is an amazing story. Your experiences make you a prime candidate for our unit. That concludes this interview. Thank you Hussain. Please follow me." Said Fletcher.

He walked to the door at the far end of the room and showed her through it to the waiting room.

George Hughes interview.

The tall, hulking shape of George Hughes took a seat in the waiting room. His blonde hair was buzz cut almost down to the skin. He wasn't much of a looker. His mouth was curled in a constant frown and he had a short stub nose. The deep scar that ran a vertical line down his left cheek didn't help his appearance. He was a formidable man who had been honed and shaped by his career. He looked at the old watch on his wrist. Although the face scratched he could still make out the time. It read 13:59. As it changed to 14:00 Fletcher opened the door.

"Mr. Hughes?"

"Yes." Said Hughes with a smile.

"Come in please."

Hughes stood up and followed Fletcher into the interview room.

"I'm Sergeant Major Fletcher. Please sit down Mr. Hughes."

Hughes sat down in the chair opposite Fletcher. As he did his eyes scanned the desk. His mind had been trained to notice every detail. The empty cup with coffee stains. The six files on the desk. Two trays. One labelled yes, the other labelled no. Three files in the yes tray, five files in the no. The four pens. Two blue, one black, one red. The desk tidy containing two pencils, one sharpener, one eraser, two rulers. One fifteen centimetres, the other thirty centimetres. All this happened in a moment. He would have taken in more but Fletcher spoke as he took Hughes' file from the pile and opened it.

"I am required by law to tell you that everything you see and hear in this room today stays in this room. If you tell anyone about anything you see or we discuss it will result in an instant court martial and dismissal from all military forces. Is that understood?"

"Yes Sir."

"I am telling you this as you already have an Official Secrets Act document in here. Some of your profiles are marked 'Top secret. Top level official clearance needed.' First of all can you start by please stating your full name, your regiment and where you are from for the record? After that tell me anything you can about yourself?" he said.

"My name is George Andrew Hughes. I am a member of the S.B.S. and other Secret Operations groups within the British military. I am from Mold in North Wales. I join the Army in 1999 and have been in the military for eighteen years. In most of that time I have been in various special operations units. I can't tell you where I have been or who I have worked with. Some of those things I don't have access to myself. I can tell you I have been trained in most land-based military exercises and operations to an expert level of understanding. I also have degrees in weapons technology and forensic science," said Hughes.

"You sound like you could be a type of person we would be willing to employ. As you must by now know you need to have had experience with a certain type of enemy to get through to this interview stage."

"Yes Sir. Vampires," Said Hughes. His mouth turning down even more than usual. "My unit had been assigned to take down a Russian warlord, Dunclar Rushkovo. He was selling military grade weapons to rebels, militias and anyone who could bid the highest price. He also dabbled in the trafficking of humans and drugs."

"Sounds like a nice guy," said Fletcher.

"Yep. He was a treat," said Hughes and continued with his story. "He owned a building in a location in Lithuania that I can't disclose. The place was active 24/7. So we watched the building for four days and noticed a pattern. Just before the sunrise and just after sunset they changed the guard. I now know that this was from vampires to humans at sunrise and human to vampires at sunset. There was a one minute window between the changeovers. One of the human guards on the eastern wall took a lot of time to unpack his personal items just after the changeover. We moved in just before sunrise. The vampire guard downed his post and just as expected the human guard took his time. We gained access through a small door that was only manned by two low level guards and entered the building. The building was an old converted warehouse. Inside there was a mess hall, sleeping quarters, the main offices and recreation areas. Our main aim was to use non-lethal force to immobilise the targets. As we swept through the building the guards were easily subdued with shock darts. We then restrained them with zip ties.
We still hadn't found Rushkovo but had seen him arrive so we knew he was in there somewhere.

We swept through the building again. Behind a block of lockers we found a hidden door which led to the basement. I took four of my soldiers down the flight of stairs that were lit with burning torches. As we made it to the bottom of the stairs it opened out into a long room. On either side of
it were cells. They were filled with naked, starved people. Some of them wept, some sat rocking back and forth and some just stared into space.
At the far end there were six people kneeling with their heads down. We moved slow and quiet into the room. This thing walked out from an alcove in the far wall. Until that day I had never seen anything like it. I'm a big man but that thing dwarfed me. Its skin was pale green and it had scales in some places.
It walked over the person on the far left, stood him up and spoke to him. They seemed to be praying. It then took hold of him, leaned his head to the side and sunk its teeth deep into his neck. We realised this was some sort of sacrifice. The man stumbled a little. The creature then dragged it clawed finger across its chest, pulled the man close, and let him drink its blood.
He fell to the floor and seemed to be having a seizure. After about twenty seconds he got back to his feet. The big thing smiled at him and moved on to the next person. I had seen enough of this. I signalled to my soldiers to change to lethal ammo and then gave them the signal to move forward. One of the women in the cells reached out and grabbed one of my soldiers by the shoulder. "Help

us," she said. That was it. A wave of panic flowed through the people.

"Help us! Help us!" they all said. They pleaded and cried.

The thing looked up and saw us. Anger contorted its features.

"Get them!" It roared.

We opened fire. I know our bullets hit the thing but they had little to no effect. A horde of guards began to pour out of the alcove behind him. The area beyond the alcove must have been huge because there must have been sixty or more of them.

We were using the most up to date armour piercing ammunition and we might as well have shot bb guns at them. They pierced the armour but it took a hell of a lot of bullets to take those guards down.

"Retreat. Retreat," I called.

We backed out to the stairs. My soldiers were torn apart and killed in moments. I turned and ran for the door. I only just got up to it and they were almost on me. As I ran out the members of my unit who were still on the ground floor gave me covering fire. The vampires just kept coming though. I've never been in a situation where my unit and I were scrabbling to get away.

The vampires moved like nothing I have ever seen. They ran over every surface and were trying to surround us faster than we could get away. They were picking us off with ease. Tough soldiers I had known for years. Well trained men and women with who I had served many missions. Yet we had no defence, nothing we could use against these monsters."

"Fall back!" I yelled.

We ran for our lives. The vampires were so close behind us I could feel their breath on the back of my neck. They were trying to cut off our exits. It was clear that I now had to make one of our own so I shot out a window.

"Go! Go!" I shouted to my soldiers.

I turned to fire a few rounds into the horde and give us chance to escape. I jumped out through the window frame. As I got to my feet and ran out into the light of the early morning sun the vampires were hesitant to follow. They stood just out of the reach of the sunlight snarling and growling. I looked round to see which of my unit had survived and found I was alone." Hughes lowered his head. When he raised his face back up and looked at Fletcher his eyes were glazed with tears. "I was low on ammunition, out gunned and outmanned. I did the only thing I could. I ran back to my rendezvous point and radioed for the pick-up. That was three month ago."

"You were lucky to make it out. I think you are more that qualified for this role. My superior officer wants to speak to you. So that concludes this interview. Thank you Hughes. Please follow me." Said Fletcher and stood up.

"Thank you," said Hughes.

He stood up to and followed Fletcher to the door at the back of the room.

"There are others in here who have passed to the next stage. You'll find food, refreshments and entertainment. Please, make yourself at home.

Adam Palmer interview.

Adam Palmer sat in the waiting room. The book he was reading looked tiny in his huge hands. His dark brown eyes moved quickly across the page. His mother had taught him to speed read at an early age in the hope that it would help him in school. In his career it had become an invaluable asset. Despite the speed he was reading he still had a habit of moving his lips while he read. The clock changed to 15.30 pm and Fletcher opened to door. The previous interviewee left.

"Adam Palmer?" Said Fletcher.

"Yes Sir," said Palmer folding the edge of the page and closing the book in one movement.

"Follow me please."

Palmer stood up and followed Fletcher into the room.

"Please take a seat Mr. Palmer. I'm Sergeant Major Fletcher."

He gestured towards the chair.

"Thank you Sir." Said Palmer and he sat down. As he did he took off his hat and rubbed his hand over the dark skin of his closely shaven head. The hat always made him itch but he always thought that formality should overcome comfort in a uniform. He looked at the desk between them. His eyes noticed everything that Hughes had done before him. He had trained in pretty much the same fields as Hughes.

Fletcher took Palmer's file from the pile and opened it.

"I see you have your Official Secrets Act documentation filled in already," he said.

"Yes. I have done this sort of work before," said Palmer.

"That will make things a lot easier. As you already know I am required by law to tell you that everything you see and hear in this room today stays in this room. If you tell anyone about anything you see or we discuss it will result in an instant court martial and dismissal from all military forces," said Fletcher.

"I understand Sir," said Palmer.

"So you're working for the government right now?"

"Yes, but I'm on leave at the moment."

"For the record please state your full name, regiment and where you are from. All for the record. Can you then tell me more about your experience in the field?"

"Sure Sir. I am Andrew William Palmer. I am a U.S. Navy Seal. I was born and still live in New York City. I started out in the U.S. Navy in 1999 at the age of eighteen. I did the basic training and spent a year serving aboard the USS Higgins. I then spent a year aboard the USS Mahan. I then transferred to the U.S. Navy Seals at the age of twenty. I was in with them for seven years. At the age of twenty seven I was headhunted for a Navy Seals black ops unit. For obvious reasons I can't relay to you what missions I was involved in, to where I was drafted, or who our targets were. I'm also a fully trained field medic, mechanic and marksman," said Palmer.

"Impressive. As I sure you already know you need to have specific experience of vampiric enemies to join this unit. Can you tell me about that please?"

"Yes Sir. It was just over a year ago. I was working in a unit in Pacific hunting smugglers of all kinds of produce, humans included. It was 18th February. 02.30am, the moon was full and visibility was high. We received word of a gang who were using speedboats to smuggle paying customers from South America into North America. We were ready and scrambled our RHIB in under five minutes."

"Sorry to interrupt but can you confirm for the recording what an RHIB is please," said Fletcher.

"Yes Sir. A Rigid Hull Inflatable Boat. A Zodiac Pro 750 Attack Boat to be exact. Our helicopter tracked them and relayed their position to us. While we were on our way the helicopter pilot instructed them to stop. Usually they throw the throttle to full and hope to outrun us. A lot of them find out the hard way that a boat can't outrun a helicopter. This gang however actually switched off their engine. We were at the location in ten minutes. The helicopter pilot told us to be careful as the gang were acting suspicious. One of them kept looking down into the hold like he was talking to someone in there. We approached with caution and hailed them with a megaphone. We went through the usual communications.

'Who are you? Why are you here? What are you carrying?'

Their responses weren't satisfactory so we decided to board them. Me and three other crewmates from our unit volunteered and as we got alongside them we stepped across onto their boat. We got them to declare their weapons and their cargo. They declared the weapons but refused to tell us what they were carrying. One of my crewmates opened the hold door and stepped down into it. He was in there for thirty seconds when there was a growl that I can only liken to a bear and a heavy thud. The door swung open and he stumbled halfway out. His left arm was completely missing. The blood was pouring out of his shoulder.

'Trap! It's a...' He said.

He was dragged back into the hold. The gang members on the deck all got a little twitchy. They bared their teeth and growled. I raised my gun and the one to my left lunged forward. I filled his face with hot lead. It took a lot to put him down. He started turning grey and fell apart when he hit the deck. That shocked the hell out of me but I didn't have time to stand and stare. I turned to the right to see one of the gang tearing a chunk of flesh from my crewmate's neck. I pulled my knife and plunged it into gang member's head. I had to stab him three times before he let go. He then looked at me right in the eye, he was still conscious and angry too. I put my hand on top of his head and dug my fingers into the wound in his skull for purchase then dragged him towards me. The wound looked like it was healing around my fingers. I pushed his head down and drove my knife into the base of his skull, where it met the spine. To a human that is a kill-switch. I had to pull and stab until his head came away from neck before he stopped moving. His body turned grey like the last guy had then crumbled apart under

34

my grip. Even his blood turned to dust. I looked over and my other crewmate had taken care of the other gang member.

'You ok?' I said.

'Yeah I'm...'

His sentence was cut short at that moment as the hold doors burst open and this huge guy came leaping out. He grabbed my crewmate by the shoulders and tore him in two like he was made of paper. Like it took him no effort at all. I was already moving. I shot at him as I jumped back across to the RIHB. Having a clear shot the rest of the crew shot at him but he just strode aboard. He knocked three of them overboard with one swing of his arm. He bent down and grabbed me. We fought but he was so much stronger than me. I don't know how I managed it but I un-holstered my sidearm and pushed it into his eye socket. I pulled the trigger and continued until the clip was empty. Somehow he was still stood up despite missing the top of his head. Then his skin turned grey and he burned from the inside out. He stumbled and then fell back into the water. His body floated for a moment then began to break apart and dissolve. My crewmates checked me over but I was fine. Just a little shook up. But hey, who wouldn't be? We towed their boat back to base and had to fill out mission reports. I did some research after that. Trying to find out what the hell those people were. That when I came across the S.O.V.E.U. A few days later I had a meeting with my Captain and told him I wanted an immediate transfer. With some reluctance he filled out the papers and got me this interview and twelve months later here I am."

"It sounds to me like you will be right at home in our organisation Mr. Palmer. That concludes this interview. Thank you," said Fletcher.

"Thank you Sir," said Palmer

Fletcher placed Palmer file in the 'Yes' tray.

"Please follow me," he said.

He then led Palmer to the door at the back of the room. "There is food, refreshments and facilities in the waiting room through here."

Lucy Mc'Ready Interview.

Lucy Mc'Ready took a seat in the waiting room. She sifted through the magazines but found nothing that interested her. She took out her phone, opened an app and started typing.

The screen lit up her green eyes. Her long red hair was tied back in a bun. Her soft, attractive features were defined by minimal makeup and bright red lipstick. She was of a slender build which was deceptive of her strength. Her long nimble fingers tapped at the phone screen until at 16.30 pm. That's when Fletcher opened the door and let out a previous interviewee.

"Miss Lucy Mc'Ready. Please come in."
She pressed the close button on the side of the phone and slipped it back into her pocket as she stood up. She then followed Fletcher into the room.

"Please have a seat Miss Mc'Ready. I am Sergeant Major Fletcher," he said.

"Thank you Sir," said Mc'Ready and sat down. Fletcher looked at her and smiled as he picked up her file.

"You're my last interview for today," he said.

"It looks like it has been a long day," she said as she looked at the 'yes' and 'no' trays.

"It has. It's been a good day though," he said and opened her file.

"I see you have signed the Official Secrets Act," said Fletcher.

"Yes Sir," said Mc'Ready.

"That's good. I am required by law to tell you that everything you see and hear in this room today stays in this room. If you tell anyone about anything you see or we discuss it will result in an instant court martial and dismissal from all military forces, is that understood?"

"Yes Sir."

"For the record please state your full name, regiment and where you are from. Then tell me about your education and military experience."

"Yes Sir. I am Lucy Sarah Mc'Ready. I am an S.A.S. Tactical and Cyber Infiltration technician. I am from Bury, North Manchester in England. I graduated from the University of Manchester with a 1:1 degrees in both computer sciences and IT development. I started working at TS Software two months later. It quickly became apparent to me that I didn't want to do that sort of work. I quit my job and enrolled in the Army in 2004. Much to the annoyance of my mum. She didn't talk to me for three weeks after I told her. She hoped that after my dad had died in Iraq in 1991 that I would have been put off. I was only six years old at the time. But the military was where I wanted to be. I completed my basic training and not long after the prospect of transferring to the S.A.S. was offered to a select few of us. I put in my transfer papers that same day. My IT and programming allowed me to excel in the four years I was in the S.A.S. I then transferred to the S.B.S. and I have worked in my unit for six years."

"So as you know, you have to have experience of a specific type of enemy. You know what I talk of."

"Yes Sir. I have fought vampires."

"Can you elaborate please, Mc'Ready?"

"It was just six weeks ago. I was on a mission in a location in Brazil the specifics of which I can't disclose. It was supposed to be quick and easy. An in and out job. We were a four person unit who specialised in target elimination. The lucky man that day was a wannabe warlord who was making big leaps up the ladder in the weapons trafficking game. He was holed up in this big old manor house. His security were more interested in playing poker than watching out for anyone, never mind infiltration units. Intelligence had told us they were hired goons. Their loyalty lay with his wallet and they would disperse as soon as they knew their money would stop.

I hacked into the electricity network, knocked out the power then we went in quiet and hard. The plan was easy, take him out and leave. It was going like clockwork. Harris, our shooter walked into the target's office a put a bullet in the guy's head. That should have been the last of it. We were making our way out of the building via a big spiral staircase when target dropped down and caught the banister. Somehow he had survived being shot point blank to the head. He reached over and grabbed West by the neck and shook him like a doll, snapping his neck. He dragged West's body over the bannister and let just him fall. With little effort he then pulled himself up on to the stairs and literally tore Simmons to pieces right there in front of us. It was horrendous. There was only me and Harris left now. We both emptied a full Diemaco C7 A2 magazine into him. He just took it all as he strode towards us. The bullets tore him and his

39

clothes but if he felt any pain he didn't show it. He reached out and grabbed Harris by the neck and proceeded to pull his throat out. We were still shooting at him when he did it. I switched to my Remington Combat Shotgun and I blew off both his feet. He fell on his back and let out this horrible scream. I can't explain the shock I felt as I watched what remained of his feet burn to ash. He lashed out towards me with clawed hands. I shot off both his arms and put my boot on his chest. He was hissing and roaring at me. I pointed the gun in his face but he put his mouth around the end of the barrel and started biting it. I tried to pull it free but his bite was like a vice. He would have crushed the end shut if I hadn't pulled the trigger and separated his head from his body. He began to burn just like his feet had.

At the time I don't know how he could be so tough. I know now that he was a vampire. I was alone in there now. My unit was gone. We had completed sixteen missions together. We were like family. I would have trusted any one of them with my life and that… that thing had just wiped them out. Like spiders under his boot." The anger and sadness were plain to see on Mc'Ready's face. Her brow furrowed and her bottom lip quivered slightly. "I had to make my own way out of there. So I started running. His goons were a lot more threatening now. It was obvious that they hadn't expected us to kill him. They thought we were walking into a trap and didn't expect any of us to survive. I suppose we all surprised each other that night.

I ran like the devil was chasing me. Right at that time I thought he was. There seemed to be a lot more of them. I had packed more flash bang grenades than I thought I would have needed. It turns out vampires don't like them at all. I found this out when I ran into what I thought was an empty room. This vamp jumped out on me. I pulled the pin from a grenade. As he ran at me I swept his legs and slammed his head into the floor. I pushed the grenade down the back of his shirt. He struggled to get up from the floor and looked at me just as the grenade went off. It literally burnt flesh from his bones, in effect cutting him in half. I made my escape by cooking the grenades for seven seconds before throwing them in to the crowd as they chased me. Eventually I got out and got to the extraction point. I had a few choice words for Intelligence when I got back to base as I suppose you can imagine.

The next day I voiced some opinions to my Captain and was informed of the existence of your organisation. The Special Operations: Vampire Elimination unit. Within two days I handed in my transfer papers and now I'm here," she said.

"You seem to like a challenge. I think you'll fit in just fine. That concludes your interview. Thank you Mc'Ready. Please follow me," said Fletcher as he placed her file in the 'yes' tray and he stood up.

"Yes Sir. Thank you Sir," she said.

He led her to the door and she followed him as they both walked through it.

The Waiting room.

They walked down a short corridor to a large room. There was a bar to the left, a seating area with magazines and books on a book shelf at the far end. In the centre there was a TV with a games console set up and to the right there was a pool table.

"Make yourself comfortable Mc'Ready. Lieutenant Colonel Andra Hudson wants to speak to you all. She's not ready yet though. The bar staff will help you if you want hot or cold drinks and food then generally relax until she is ready."

"Thank you Sir," said Mc'Ready.

"Ok. Have fun," he said and made his way to the bar.

She looked around. She didn't know any of these people yet but that would come with time.

White and Davis were sat at the bar talking, Hughes and Palmer were playing a racing game on the games console, and Hussain was stood at the pool table setting up the balls.

"Hi. I'm Zarveya. Fancy a game?" She said to Mc'Ready.

"Yes, sure. Hi, I'm Lucy Mc'Ready."

"Watch her. She plays a mean game." Said Palmer without looking away from the TV screen.

"Hey, don't scare her away." Said Hussain with a smile.

Mc'Ready laughed.

"What rules are we playing?" She said.

Andra's Welcome.

Twenty minutes passed and the door opened. A tall woman walked in. She was six feet six inches tall and dressed in a slim, grey trouser suit. She spoke with an air of confidence and authority that only comes with an immense sense of self belief.

"Hello. May I have your undivided attention?" She said.
They all stopped what they were doing and looked at her. Some of them looked shocked while others tried to hide their reaction.

Her skin was purple and covered in tiny, smooth scales and her eyes were solid green. She looked almost reptilian except for her blonde hair. It was long, wavy, and sheened under the lights. Her features were unusual but beautiful in an odd way.

"At ease soldiers. I am Lieutenant Colonel Andra Hudson. I am Head of The Special Operations: Vampire Elimination unit. Yes, your eyes do not deceive you. This is how I look. I'm sure you have many questions. We will get to that. At least you now know why you had to sign the official secrets act. This is no ordinary unit. You have all passed the medical, intelligence, fitness, weapons and interview stages of your application. I want to welcome you aboard personally."
They were awestruck for moment, then they all stepped forwards, stood to attention and saluted. White spoke first,

"Ma'am, forgive our reaction. It was not our intention to offend."
She smiled at him,

"At ease soldiers. I know you didn't. I've had more than enough time to get used to people staring. You're not the first and you all definitely won't be the last. I know how I look and I know it is a surprise to most people. So please relax," she said.

"Yes Ma'am," they all said.

"You have got to this point because though you found yourselves in situations where your friends, family and colleagues died. Yet you all survived being attacked by vampires. All those vampires are connected by one main vampire. The first and strongest of their kind. Their Lord Ruhsarr. The mission statement of the S.O.V.E.U. is to crush the vampires. With our main aim being to hunt down and kill Ruhsarr. All the applicants who were interviewed are now part of the S.O.V.E.U. You will not only be part of this unit. You are my personal attack team. You take orders from me and your superiors. However when I deem it necessary you will take orders from me and me alone. You will perform these orders to the best of your ability. I had Fletcher hand-pick you from the applicants. You are all members now. I just have just one more question. Do you belong here?"

"I think we do Ma'am. We got all the way through the interview stage. So yes. I think we all belong here," said Hughes.

"You think? You think you belong here? The question was do you belong here. So… do you belong here?"

The interviewees looked at one and another then back at Andra and said,

"Yes Ma'am."

"I can't hear you! Do you belong here?!" she said.

"Yes Ma'am!" they all said.

"Atttteeention!"

They all stood to attention and Andra saluted them and they all saluted back.

"White, Davis, Hughes, Hussain, Palmer, Mc'Ready. Welcome to my unit," said Andra with a big smile.

"Thank you Ma'am," said the new recruits in unison.

The adventures of Andra Hudson and the
S.O.V.E.U. will continue in the forthcoming novel
'Beasts of Immortality'.

About the Author:

Paul James Kearns is an indie author from Bolton, a town in the North West of England. He lives there with Carrie and their two children.

He has always written from an early age. He started to take his writing serious when he met Carrie who supports him, even when he is ranting about his weird and wonderful character's adventures.

He would like to thank you, the reader, for buying this book and supporting him.

I hope you enjoyed reading this novelette as much as Paul obviously enjoyed writing it. Maybe it has given you a bit of inspiration to write your own stories too.

Thank you and happy reading.

Other books by Paul J Kearns:
The Hunted and other Twisted Tales.

You can find Paul J Kearns on social media.
Facebook: Facebook.com/PJKearnsAuthor
Instagram: pauljkearnsauthor
Twitter: @pjkearnsauthor
Wordpress: Pauljkearns.wordpress.com

Printed in Poland
by Amazon Fulfillment
Poland Sp. z o.o., Wrocław

62154496R00031